Merry Moosey Christmas

Written by
Lynn Plourde

Illustrated by
Russ Cox

For Lynn, Nate, and Alissa
–RUSS COX

With love to Kaida, who has made my life more merry
–LYNN PLOURDE

Published by Islandport Press
P.O. Box 10
Yarmouth, Maine 04096
books@islandportpress.com
www.islandportpress.com

Third printing, 2016

ISBN: 978-1-939017-38-3
Library of Congress Control Number: 2013958205
Printed in Canada by Friesens Book Division
Production Date: October 2016
Job #: 227493

Merry Moosey Christmas

Written by
Lynn Plourde

Illustrated by
Russ Cox

Everyone deserves a holiday break.

“Please, Santa, pleeeeease,” begged Rudolph.
“Just this once, can’t I pleeeeeease have Christmas Eve off?”

Santa looked skeptical.

Rudolph persisted.

“I’ve never had a chance to stay home on Christmas Eve and listen for jingling sleigh bells on the roof and a *whoooooosh* down the chimney with presents just for **me**!”

Santa's heart was as soft as his belly.

"Ho-ho-ho," he laughed. "Okay, Rudy, just this once. But first we **must** find a worthy replacement to lead my sleigh on the most special night of the year, and **you** must help me train him."

And so Santa and Rudolph set off in search of the perfect substitute.

“What about him?” asked Santa.
“Wrong size,” said Rudolph.

“How about that one?” Santa pointed.
“Too feathery,” said Rudolph.

“Antlers?” asked Santa.
“Horns,” said Rudolph.

Discouraged, Santa and Rudolph flew northward.

“Sorry, Rudy,” said Santa. “It looks like you won’t get Christmas Eve off after all.”

“Whoa! Wait! What’s that?” exclaimed Rudolph.

They landed the sleigh at the edge of a forest.

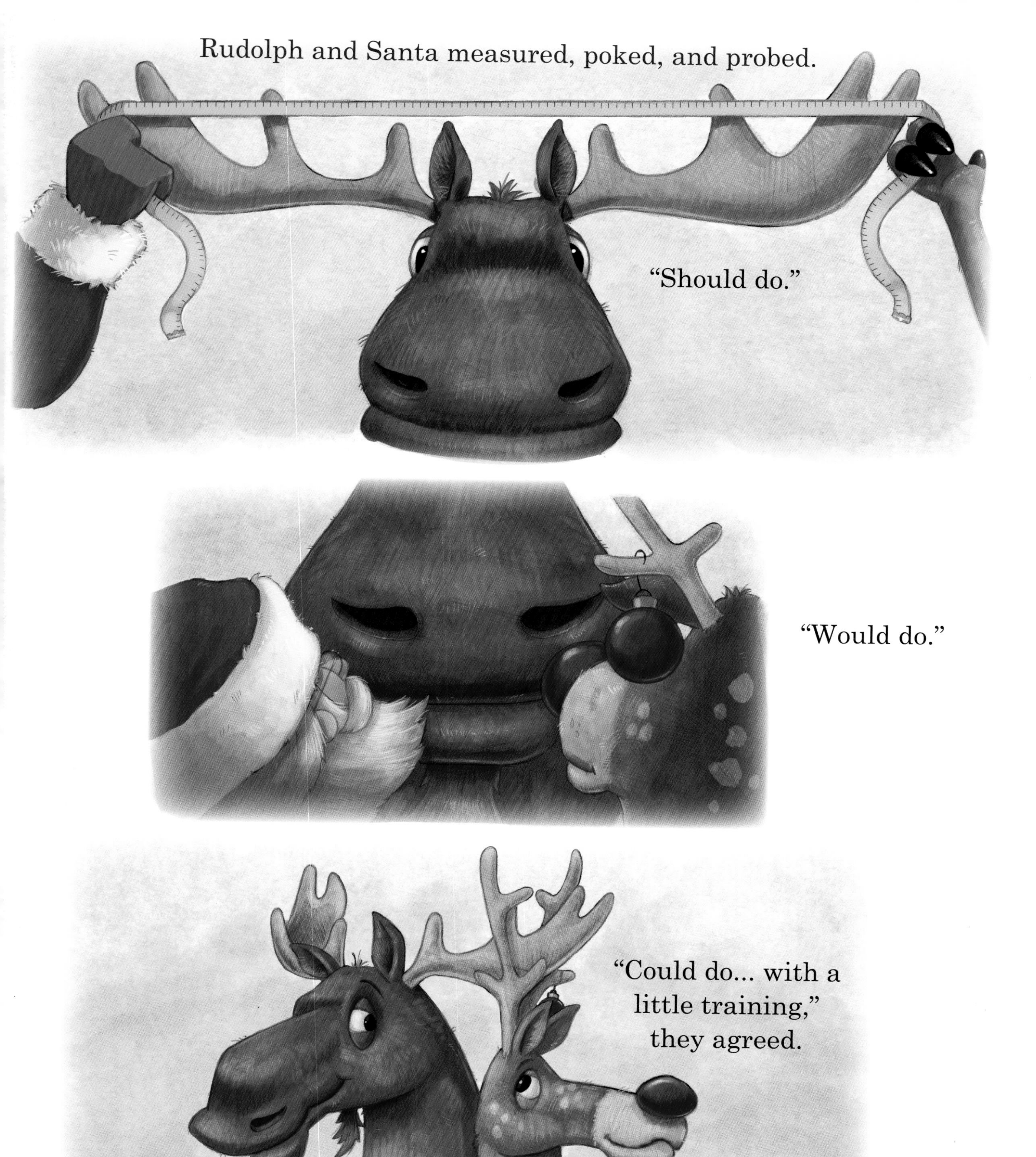

Rudolph and Santa measured, poked, and probed.

"Should do."

"Would do."

"Could do... with a little training," they agreed.

The moose seemed willing.

"What should we teach him first?" asked Santa. "Nose glowing," answered Rudolph.

Rudolph stood in front of the moose and made his nose glow—*flashity-flash-flash*. "Now you try it," said Rudolph. "Just think BRIGHT thoughts."

The moose thought of hot sunny days and car headlights. He grunted, groaned, held his breath, and stood on his head until his face turned red, but his nose didn't glow.

"Maybe this'll work." Santa offered a clown nose out of his sack. Rudolph shook his head. "Sorry, Santa. It looks funny and doesn't really shine."

The moose held up a hoof, as if to say, "Wait a minute," and raced down the road.

He was back in a flash, wearing a headlamp.

"That's not a nose," said Santa.

"Shines plenty of light," said Rudolph, "to help you find your way."

"It'll do," Santa and Rudolph agreed.

"What's next?" asked Santa.

"Flying," answered Rudolph.

Rudolph took a few flying leaps over the moose's head —*leapity-leap-leap*.

"Now you try it," said Rudolph. "Just think SOARING thoughts."

The moose thought of gliding eagles and floatplanes taking off from the lake. The moose stood on his back tippy toes and flapped his front legs while Rudolph gave him a boost. But he didn't lift off the ground one itty-bitty bit.

“Maybe this’ll work.” Out of his sack, Santa pulled a beanie cap with a propeller.

Rudolph shook his head. “Sorry, Santa. That looks silly, and it would take a much **bigger** propeller to lift that big fella.”

The moose held up a hoof, as if to say, “Wait a minute,” and raced down the road again.

This time he whizzed back with a jetpack.

Santa and Rudolph looked at each other and agreed, “It’ll do.”

“What’s next?” asked Santa.

“Directions,” answered Rudolph.

Rudolph gave a lecture on the North Star, latitude and longitude, traveling through time zones—*yakity-yak-yak*.

“Now you try it,” said Rudolph. “Just think GUIDING thoughts.”

The moose thought of hunters’ compasses and signs telling out-of-staters where to go. The moose pointed north with his snout, south with his antlers, east with his front legs, and west with his back legs.

“Maybe this will help.” Santa pulled a globe out of his sack.

“Sorry, Santa,” said Rudolph. “He’ll need more detail to find streets and addresses.”

The moose held up a hoof, as if to say, “Wait a minute,” and raced down the road.

He found his way back with a GPS strapped to his antlers.

Santa and Rudolph nodded. "It'll do."

“What’s next?” asked Santa.

Rudolph thought out loud, “ Let’s see . . . nose glowing, flying, directions . . . seems like there’s one more thing. But I can’t remember what it is.”

“Couldn’t be too important, then,” said Santa.

“Well, if I think of it, I’ll let you know,” Rudolph told the moose. “In the meantime, practice, practice, practice, and arrive at the North Pole at dusk on Christmas Eve, ready to go.”

“Thanks, Moosey,” added Santa, giving the moose a pat.

Santa and Rudolph headed back to the North Pole where they were busy, busy, busy getting ready for Christmas Eve.

The moose stayed home where he was dizzy, dizzy, dizzy getting ready for Christmas Eve.

The moose couldn't help himself. He was soooooooo anxious, he arrived at the North Pole at dawn on Christmas Eve Day.

He tried to stay out of the way while Santa, Rudolph, the elves, and the other reindeer finished all the final preparations for the **big** night.

Rudolph stayed with the sleigh until the last second, making certain everything was perfect.

"Not having second thoughts about staying home this year, are you, Rudy?" asked Santa.

Rudolph gulped a big gulp, leaned over, and whispered, “Doesn’t matter if I were. Look how excited the big guy is to have a turn leading your sleigh.”

“You’re right.” Santa winked. “But still, it won’t be the same without you.”

Rudolph turned for home before more than his nose turned red.

At last, it was time to go.

"Giddy-UP!" shouted Santa.

The moose soared skyward.

Santa ordered, "To Rudy's house first, Moosey.
He's been waiting a lifetime for this special night.
We mustn't keep him waiting."

The moose flew to Rudolph's, straight and steady.

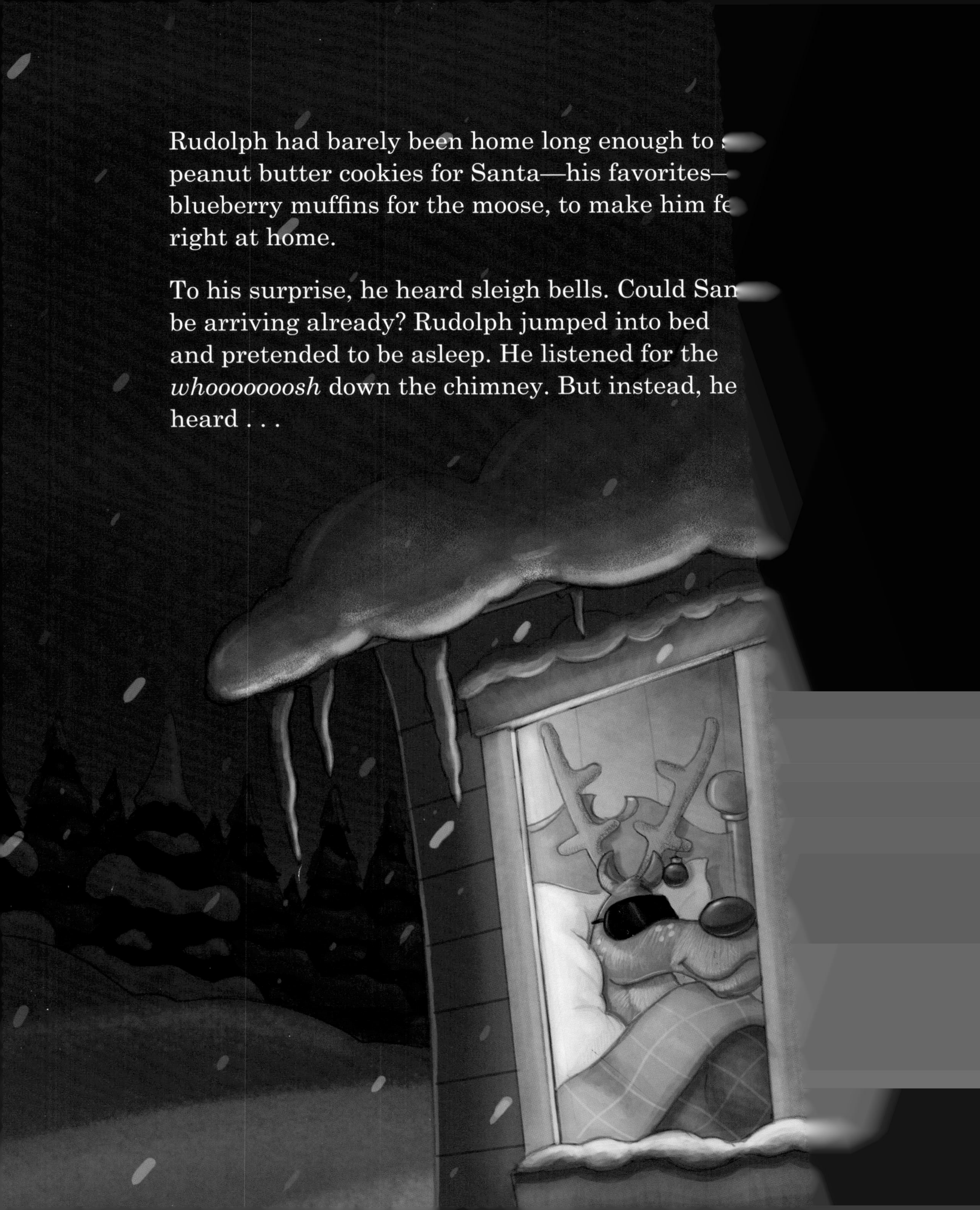

Rudolph had barely been home long enough to s
peanut butter cookies for Santa—his favorites—
blueberry muffins for the moose, to make him fe
right at home.

To his surprise, he heard sleigh bells. Could San
be arriving already? Rudolph jumped into bed
and pretended to be asleep. He listened for the
whoooooooosh down the chimney. But instead, he
heard . . .

CRASH!
BANG!

BOOM!

Rudolph jumped out of bed and looked up the chimney.

Santa rolled out of the sled and looked down the chimney.

They shouted, **“Landings!** We forgot to teach him how to do landings!”

Rudolph hurried onto the roof and helped to right the sleigh.

But before he could utter a word on how to do landings, the moose held up a hoof as if to say, "Wait a min..."

Rudolph interrupted, "I know. Climb in. I'll take you."

Rudolph jetted the sleigh back to Moosey's favorite store.

"They'll do," Santa and Rudolph agreed.

"Hurry! There's no time to waste. Millions of kids are counting on you," Rudolph shouted.

Santa snapped the reins, and the sleigh lifted off, with Moosey leading the way.

And that Christmas Eve, some pretending-to-be-asleep children not only heard jingling sleigh bells and a *whooooooosh* down the chimney, but also . . .

"MERRY MOOSEY CHRISTMAS
to all and
to all, a good night!"